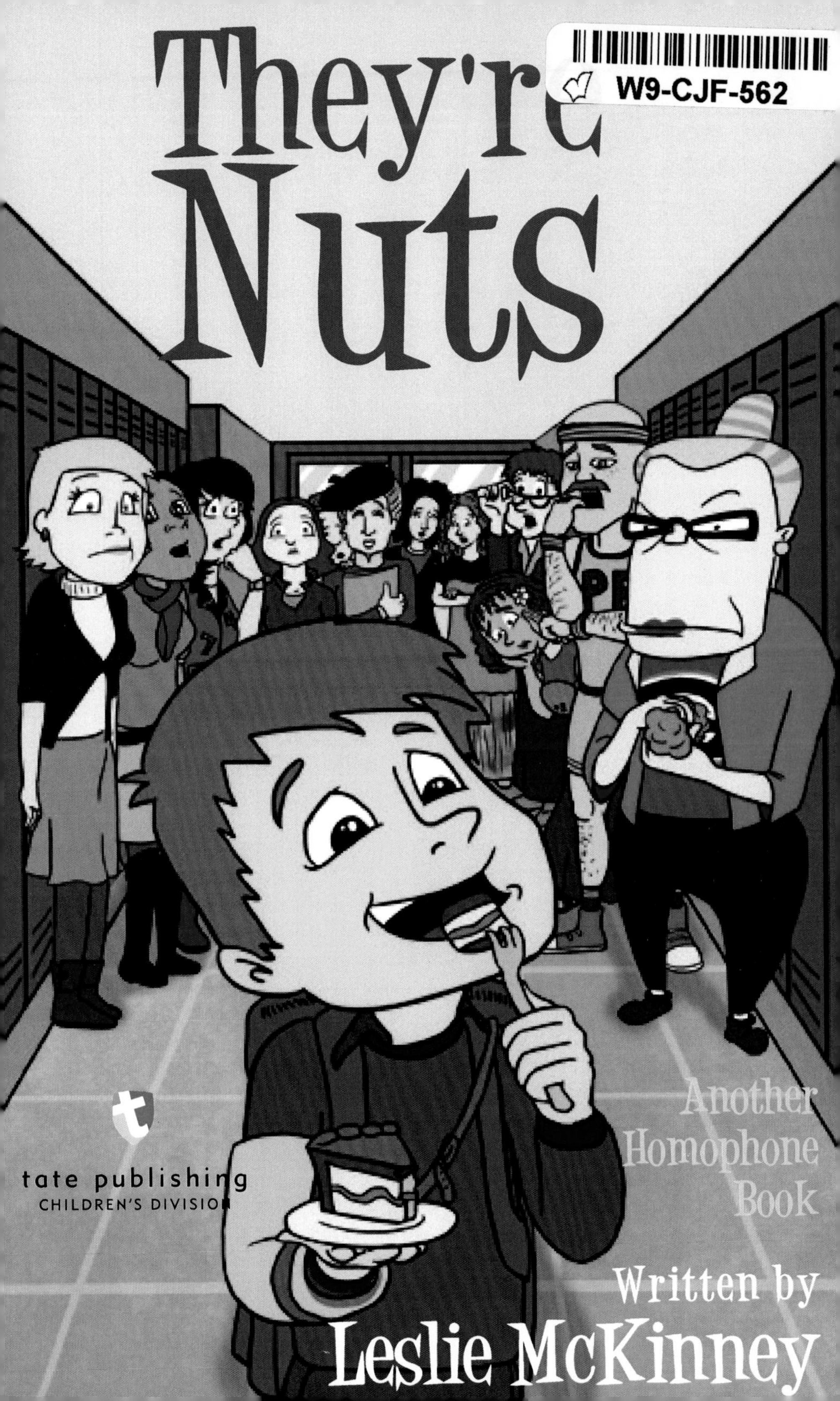

They're Nuts
Another Homophone Book
Written by Leslie McKinney
tate publishing
CHILDREN'S DIVISION

This title is also available as a Tate Out Loud product. Visit www.tatepublishing.com for more information.

Published by Tate Publishing & Enterprises, LLC
127 E. Trade Center Terrace | Mustang, Oklahoma 73064 USA
1.888.361.9473 | www.tatepublishing.com

Tate Publishing is committed to excellence in the publishing industry. The company reflects the philosophy established by the founders, based on Psalm 68:11,
"The Lord gave the word and great was the company of those who published it."

Cover and interior design by James Mensidor
Illustrations by Dindo Contento

Published in the United States of America

ISBN: 978-1-63268-737-1
Juvenile Fiction / General
14.06.10

This book is dedicated to my generous and genuine son, Parker McKinney. Your huge heart keeps mine full. I love you!

Mom

Acknowledgments

I would like to thank the following people for being another set of eyes, giving advice, and helping me revise, revise, revise:

Julie Rosenkranz, Amy Rubin, Einat Shinar, Jinny Carter, Dave and Sheri Brown.

And a very special thanks to all of the teachers who are in this book and who are not. You have shaped the lives of Will and Parker and so many other children. Know that what you do is so very important and that you are treasures!

Thank you, thank you, thank you!

And thank you for helping us all enjoy reading a little more by teaching us the fun of figurative language!

Terms of Figurative Language

Hyperbole

A figure of speech that uses exaggeration for emphasis.

Ex: “It was so cold I nearly froze to death!”

Simile

A figure of speech that compares two unlike things directly, using the words like or as.

Ex: “My fingers felt like icicles.”

Metaphor

A figure of speech that compares two unlike things directly, without the use of like or as.

Ex: “My fingers were icicles.”

Idiom

A figure of speech whose meaning is not predictable from the usual meanings of the words used in it.

Ex: “It’s raining cats and dogs.”

Despite his many dangerous mishaps, Parlous Parker finally made it to fourth grade! He had always liked or disliked school as much as any other kid. But after his first day of fourth grade, he came home and announced to his mother that he was never going back. “Why not?” his mother asked. “Because *they’re* nuts!” he exclaimed. “You were all fired up this morning. What happened at school today?” his mother asked. And he told her.

Right when I got to school, I met my new homeroom teacher, Ms. Hound Dawg Hayes. She talked a mile a minute. My head was spinning immediately. She said that fourth grade was a whole new world and that we were going to soar to new heights. She said we’d have a different teacher for each class, but not to worry because we could handle it. She said our brains are like sponges and that as long as we keep filling them, *they’ll* keep absorbing. *WHAT?* My brain feels plenty full right now. I like the world I live in, and I’m afraid of heights! I was ready right then and *there* to go home...but I stayed. I really think I learned all of the important things I need to know from Ms. Easygoing Ellsworth in kindergarten: Be nice, Be helpful, Be a problem solver, Read, and Share. Isn’t that all I really need to know? “Can’t I just stay home, Mom?” he asked.

“Oh, it doesn’t sound too bad so far. Tell me more,” she said.

I had Mrs. Cordial Connors for social studies. She smiled and taught us about citizenship and how our forefathers said we were all created equal. She said that we all have certain unalienable rights: life, liberty, and the pursuit of happiness. I wasn't sure why we were talking about aliens, but I was ready right then and *there* to take the liberty of coming home to pursue my happiness right here on the couch...but obviously, I didn't. I stayed *there*.

Next, I went to Ms. Meticulous Martin's room for math. She said that numbers are everywhere! *They're* NOT! She also said that *there* is a time and place for everything and that in her class *there* is no time to play. She said it was time to get serious about our education. I was seriously thinking it was time to go home...but I stayed *there*.

Sweet Ms. Sweeney was my science teacher. But even *there* we were reminded that *there's* a process for everything! She also said it's good to question things. So, I asked a question... "When is recess?" She informed me that it was right after my language arts class. If it hadn't been soon, I may have left the building.

PERIODIC TABLE of ELEMENTS
THE SCIENTIFIC METHOD
Ask QUESTION
Research
HYPOTHESIS
EXPERIMENT
Analysis

Swift Ms. Sgroe taught language arts and it flew by like a hurricane. She read to us the whole time and it seemed like we were only *there* for a split second, and then we were free!

RECESS! It was a good thing it was time for recess because my brain was on overload and about to explode!

At least we did get some perks with all the responsibility *they're* giving us. We can go here and *there* and everywhere on the playground now. I guess *there* is an upside to being responsible. But *they're* still way too serious about the fourth grade.

When I went to lunch, I realized for the first time that I wasn't going see Wild Will in *there* anymore now that he's moved on to middle school. I wondered about what *they're* eating at his school. I heard they get to pick *their* own lunch line in middle school and that the food is to die for! I guess I also realized that I'm actually going to miss him being *there*. Please don't tell him I said that!

After I'd had recess and lunch, my day was getting a little better, but the teachers were still nutty. We actually got to meet all of our "specials" teachers today.

My art teacher, Ms. Awesome Andrews, was out of this world! I mean that literally. Actually, I think all art teachers are in a world of *their* own. She talked about Petrini, Padmini, Pezzati... *Who does she think she's talking to, Picasso?* I hope she wasn't talking to me because I didn't understand a word she said. I thought we were just supposed to draw and paint and make things in *there*.

PE

In PE, Crazy Coach Short was a machine today! He was bending over backwards to get us excited about exercising. They all were! They said the reason for all *their* excitement was that they didn't want us to become couch potatoes. Speaking of couches, I could hear mine calling me...but I stayed *there*.

The computer lab teacher really threw me for a loop! Mrs. Capricious Cruz said that while we were in *there*, we could drive on the technology highway of the world! Then, she said that we could *not* surf freely, but that we had to follow certain guidelines. While she was talking about driving and surfing, I was thinking about catching a ride or a wave home, but I didn't...I stayed *there*. *There's* no telling what she'll say tomorrow.

SCHOOL BUS

Music class almost made me want to stay! Miss Fabulous Flynn was as mellow as a mushroom and at the same time electric! And Ms. Delightful Davidson was as cool as a cucumber. It was like they were conducting a symphony instead of teaching fourth graders how to keep up with a beat and grow up at the same time. I think *there* is something special about music teachers. *They're* yummy nuts!

Seniorita Skeens taught me a little Spanish today, "*No somos coco locos.*" It's fun to say, and do you know what that means? It means, "We're not crazy coconuts." I didn't tell her that I thought all of my teachers were crazy coconuts.

I started thinking everything was going to be all right, and then it happened...My planner disappeared! I just knew someone must have taken it! I know I didn't do anything with it. It was right *there*! Or over *there*? I didn't know where it was or who took it. I looked everywhere around me and it was nowhere to be found. I was about to lose my mind looking for it. Then, Ms. Hayes suggested that I retrace my steps. Even though I knew she was nuts and that I didn't lose it, I did what she said; first, I went to Ms. Martin's room, then Ms. Sweeney's room. After that, I went to Ms. Sgroe's room and just as I was about to lose all hope of finding it, *there* it was–in the seat I was sitting in when I was in *there*. It's weird how it got back *there*.

“Mom, by the end of the day I had total brain drain. I don’t think I can do this anymore. I’m not ready for all this! I’m only 9 years old and *they’re* treating me like I’m 19. Like I said before, *they’re* nuts! I’m not going back.”

“Well,” said his mother, “I know you and I know what you can do. You weren’t expecting all of this, but you can handle it! Change is hard, but necessary. Now that you know how things are, tomorrow will be much easier. I promise. The first day of change is always the hardest. You march in *there* tomorrow, step up to the plate, rise to the challenge, and knock *their* socks off!”

He did! Parker’s second day was a piece of cake and he had an amazing fourth grade year with all of those wonderfully nutty teachers.

This story is full of figurative language. Can you find one example of each of these types?

simile:

metaphor:

idiom:

hyperbole:

Choose one to illustrate:

listen|imagine|view|experience

AUDIO BOOK DOWNLOAD INCLUDED WITH THIS BOOK!

In your hands you hold a complete digital entertainment package. In addition to the paper version, you receive a free download of the audio version of this book. Simply use the code listed below when visiting our website. Once downloaded to your computer, you can listen to the book through your computer's speakers, burn it to an audio CD or save the file to your portable music device (such as Apple's popular iPod) and listen on the go!

How to get your free audio book digital download:

1. Visit www.tatepublishing.com and click on the e|LIVE logo on the home page.
2. Enter the following coupon code:
   5934-9d7c-8145-8464-3978-2da8-c2d7-8754
3. Download the audio book from your e|LIVE digital locker and begin enjoying your new digital entertainment package today!